The Chronicles of Timothy Tabbis

The Unlikely Friendship Between
Timothy Tabbis and Randolph Robin

The Chronicles of Timothy Tabbis

The Unlikely Friendship Between Timothy Tabbis and Randolph Robin

Stephan Collins

Illustrated by Arlan DeRussy

Illustrated by Arlan DeRussy

ISBN: 978-0-557-09266-6

Contents

Chapter 1

Three Blue Eggs

Professor Bewilly pressed firmly on the top lip of the window and pushed upward. It stubbornly resisted but eventually gave a foot of opening. He judged it to be enough, turned out the light, and sleepily climbed the stairs, while making a mental list of last-minute things to pack.

The early morning sky was a deep ocean blue. Out of the cool shadows a large feline figure bounded onto the window's ledge. In one silky motion it slipped through the ample opening just as a tall slender silhouette appeared in the dim doorway. Professor Bewilly, still in his night robe, yawned, stretched his long arms, plopped down into the large leather chair facing the window, and softly said, "Good morning my dear old friend, good to have you home again." Then through thin lips he added, "And just in the nick of time."

"We're going on a journey . . . crossing the pond to America, to a place called the Kickapoo River Valley."

He gazed affectionately at the large tabby, sitting statuesque on the window ledge. "Tim, what do you . . . " he began, but stopped before finishing. "Oh begging your pardon, sir," he said with a smile in his voice, "what do you think, Timothy Tabbis?"

At the sound of his full name, Timothy Tabbis, the big yellow tabby cat, raised his almond eyes and jumped the gap from window ledge to the professor's lap. He raised himself upon his hind legs, resting his very large front paws on the professor's chest, and looked at him squarely.

"Yes, you heard right," Professor Bewilly said, as if detecting a question in his furry friend's inquisitive gaze, "We're going on a journey."

The big cat purred and nuzzled his sleek forehead between the professor's cupped hands as if to say *I'll go anywhere with you.* Playfully the professor pulled on his friend's larger than usual pointy ears, but the big cat shook loose. His emerald eyes twinkled in the early rays of sunlight spilling over the big leather chair, and Professor Bewilly whispered, "Journey, just another word for adventure."

On the branch of a maple tree at the edge of a lush forest lived two birds, Pete and Pattie Robin. Their nest overlooked the sloping hills

of the Kickapoo River Valley in southwestern Wisconsin. Pete landed next to their nest with a juicy worm and gave it to Pattie.

"Do you think it will be soon? Are there any signs yet? Why is it taking so long?"

"No, not yet dear. You can't rush these sorts of things. Be patient," said Pattie.

The next day Pete and Pattie left their maple tree in search of worms. But this would not be just another ordinary day; for the winds carried nature's beckoning to their unborn chicks. They pushed and nudged, nudged and pushed, until the first, then the second, and finally the last little beak broke through its turquoise shell.

Pete and Pattie were overjoyed when they returned to find three little wonderful chicks, one girl and two boys.

"What shall we name them?" asked Pattie.

Rubbing his beak, Pete said, "Well, this one we'll call Ruby. I can see she'll be quite a jewel." He scratched his head as he looked at the next one, and said, "This one we'll call Robby, after my father, I can see he'll be a chip off the ole block." But when he came to the last one he squinted, folded his wings one over the other, and patted his foot. Finally he said, "This one . . . let me see. This one . . . we'll call him . . . Randolph. Yes, Randolph."

"Those are marvelous names," agreed Pattie, as she and Pete gazed affectionately upon their featherless chicks.

And like all babies they kept their mother and father busy from sunrise to sunset feeding their bottomless tummies. *More food, we're hungry, more food* they demanded, as their cherry round heads bobbed atop outstretched necks. It wasn't long before the three baby robins waddled upright on fat little bellies exploring the world around them through large playful eyes.

One day Ruby joked, "Robby, there's a spider on your head."

Robby yelled, "Get it off. Get it off."

"She's just pulling your wing," laughed Randolph.

Their bodies were soon covered with tiny fluffs, a sign it would not be long before their big day.

"Children, watch closely," said Pattie. "I will demonstrate how to exercise your muscles for your upcoming flight day." She stood tall, lifted her rust-colored breast and, using her tail feathers for balance, gracefully flapped her wings making the air swish and swirl. "Now it's your turn. Stand straight. Use your tail feathers to help you balance and begin flapping. Ruby, you first."

Ruby and Robby did well. They lifted their chests, balanced their slender tail feathers, and worked their wings as Pattie demonstrated. But for Randolph, things did not go so well. When his right wing was flapping, his left did nothing. When he got his left going, his right wing stopped. And if that wasn't bad enough, his short and stubby tail feathers were of no help at all.

"That's great, Randolph. You can do it," Pattie called out from the edge of the nest. "Keep up the good work." Nevertheless, no matter how much she praised him, Randolph ended up tipping over.

"Oh, don't worry," she said as she helped him to his feet. "Everyone has trouble in the beginning."

"But mom," grumbled Randolph, "Ruby and Robby aren't."

Pattie hugged him, "You know, Randolph, I bet you'll do things no other robin has ever done, so don't give up. One day you will fly, I promise."

Determined to keep up with Robby and Ruby, he practiced harder and longer day after day, only to end up on his back.

One night as their chicks slept Pete paced along their branch. "How can he," he said in a troubled whisper, "fly without tail feathers?"

Pattie moved closer to him as his lament melted into the constant chirping of crickets, the swooping flutter of bat wings, and the occasional hollow hoot of an owl hunting the black forest floor.

"It's hard to know what to do," she replied, "but we must not let him get discouraged."

Pete nodded, and said, "Yes, you're right."

One lazy afternoon while the three babies napped, Randolph awoke to the cackling of their neighbors, two cantankerous but lovable old crows, Myrtle and Pauline.

"Pauline," Myrtle said, "did you see that incredible right turn Maybelle made the other day?"

"Yes, I did," replied Pauline. "Why, if it weren't for her terrific skills and correct use of her tail feathers she would have landed head first into that thorn bush."

The two old friends laughed at the thought, looked at each other, and crowed, "May you always have the wind at your back and a great set of tail feathers to steer you in."

In one great swoosh, first one then the other, the two old friends took to the sky, and Randolph was left to wonder.

During the evening hours the birds that could not fly high or far searched the ground for bugs and seeds. The three young robins stopped their play to watch and listen as they passed below.

"Connie," gobbled Lulu the turkey, "What do you think of Tom? Isn't he absolutely dashing when he fans out those marvelous tail feathers?"

"Mmm . . . mmm . . . mmm," gobbled Connie, "what a turkey."

Randolph could not help but admire these flightless creatures. What they lacked they made up for with style, each displaying a lush fan of tail feathers. Randolph looked back at his short crop of plumes and wished for a miracle. He wished one day he too would have the wind at his back and a strong set of tail feathers to steer him in. He thought *if only I had tail feathers like theirs.*

Chapter 2

Rise and Fall

"Rule number three." Pete always started with the last rule first. "No pushing. Rule number two, take turns. There's room for only one flapper at a time. And rule number one. This is the most important one for you to remember. Never, *ever* practice on the edge of the nest."

"Why?" chirped Ruby.

"Because beyond the nest," began Pete, "there is gravity, and gravity will pull you down where we cannot help you. Leaving you at the mercy of . . . " He paused to give more drama to the word, "cats!"

"Dad, what's gra . . . gra . . . ?" interrupted Randolph.

"Gravity," Pete instructed.

"Remember the other day when a leaf fell into our nest?"

"Yes!" Randolph exclaimed.

Pete smiled and said, "Well, it was gravity that made the leaf fall."

"But if . . . if the leaf had wings . . . " Randolph said thoughtfully.

"Very good Randolph, you got it," said Pete. "If the leaf had wings, it would never have fallen in our nest. It would have flown away."

Robby quickly piped in, "What are cats?"

Dramatically rising to the tips of his toes and puffing out his chest, he explained, "Cats are big furry animals with four legs, long tails, and a mouth full of sharp teeth."

Ruby nervously asked, "What do we . . . do . . . if we see one?"

Pete wrinkled his brow. "There are three rules you must remember if you ever cross the path of a cat. Rule number three. They'll make a meal of you if given half the chance. Rule number two. Once in sight, take flight. And rule number one. If it's too late for flight, hide from sight." He then opened his wings to their full expanse, glanced over his shoulder, and winked. "It's worked for me on many occasions." Then off he flew to join Pattie on another day's hunt.

Randolph, Robby, and Ruby were eager to start their daily exercises.

Ruby went first. She checked her tail feathers for balance. Pushed her chest upward, and gradually pumped her wings. What happened next, words could not express. Randolph and Robby looked at each other with eyes as big as walnuts as Ruby lifted upward.

"It's like magic," she spouted. However, she lost her concentration and softly plopped down into the nest.

"My turn. It's my turn," exclaimed Robby.

Following Ruby's example he too rose and, for four incredible seconds, he felt the magic of flight before plunking back into the nest.

Robby and Ruby nudged Randolph to the center of the nest.

"Your turn, Randolph," said Ruby.

"You can do it," said Robby.

"Oh, oh, oh . . . I . . . I . . . I don't know if I can," stuttered Randolph.

"Yes you can," Ruby and Robby replied in unison.

So Randolph did as his brother and sister had done. He began working his wings as best he could.

"You're doing great, Randolph," cheered Ruby.

"Yeah, you're really looking good," shouted Robby.

The air began swirling like a tiny storm, sending small bits of nest upward. Randolph was beginning to feel like maybe he could fly.

Ruby and Robby did not notice how close Randolph had come to the edge of the nest.

Then all at once everything started going wrong. Randolph's right wing stopped flapping. His left wing kind of sped up, and as usual his tail feathers were of no use. He stumbled backward and fell out of the nest!

"Where'd he go?" Robby asked.

"I don't know," answered Ruby.

"Hey you guys, where are you?" A small far away voice called from below.

Ruby and Robby inched their way to the nest edge. "We're here. Where are you?"

"I think I'm on the ground," Randolph replied.

"How did you get down there?" chirped Robby.

"I think . . . grabity got me," Randolph said sadly.

"Well, you better get back up here before mom and dad get home," insisted Ruby, "or we all will be in big trouble."

"Try flying," urged Robbie.

Randolph was about to try when not far up the path the silhouette of a creature came into view.

Ruby called out, "Randolph! Stop! There's something coming."

"What is it?" chirped Randolph.

Ruby tried to stay calm, "Well . . . it has four legs."

"A tail," added Robby.

"And fur," whispered Ruby.

"Hide from sight!!!" yelled Robby.

Fortunately, Randolph had landed near a hollow log. He quickly hopped inside and waited for the coast to clear.

Chapter 3

Timothy Tabbis Meets Randolph

Timothy Tabbis and Professor Bewilly's new home was a quaint little farm house surrounded by the hills of the Kickapoo River Valley. The professor spent the first week putting their home in order while the big yellow cat explored its every nook and cranny. But the urge to roam was building in Timothy Tabbis. By week's end he

impatiently lingered on the ledge of the study window. As Professor Bewilly organized his bookshelves, he glanced over his wire rim spectacles, saddled on the lower bridge of his long narrow nose, and said, "Ready to go, huh?"

The golden tabby padded silently beneath broad ferns of the adjacent woods stirring the alarmed chirps and chatter of birds and squirrels. Soon the excited clamor faded to watchful eyes. When the arching ferns gave way to the woodland vista

Timothy Tabbis stopped to feast his gaze on its peaceful beauty. "What splendor," he said aloud, as he looked up into the vast emerald canopy above him and an endless carpet of moist earth and growth before him. And as he stood in admiration there arose a cool current of air wafting a peculiar scent, which his keen sense of smell did not miss. As always, an interesting aroma prompted a look-see.

The scent led him out of the cool shade of the forest and into a sundrenched valley. The murky water of the Kickapoo River soundlessly snaked through the valley, carving elbow turns and gentle curves, as though confused about which direction it would venture. As he explored its twist and bends he was inspired to compose a traveling song. Something he enjoyed doing when out in the wild.

"Cats are lazy . . . " he began, "cats are crazy . . . " he added but hesitated. Then these words came to him, "Cats are fast, cats are quick, cats jump higher than a pogo stick. Cats are clean with their furry sheen, sitting in the lap of a British Queen."

He eventually tired of the river's unpredictable course and headed for the hills overlooking the river where trees loomed as high as the sky. Though the landscape was unfamilar, he navigated its ancient hills and ravines with the ease and stealth of his kind, and with each step he felt a kinship with its wildness.

While exploring the steep slopes and high ridges of this wonderous landscape he sighted a far off glen. Upon reaching its secluded realm he could hear the constant march of a running stream. Unlike the river it never strayed from its course through the forest, as it gushed over large stones and boulders. He drank, licked his whiskers, then turned to leave. But the glint of somethng moving beneath the underbrush caught his attention. The possibility of a delicacy he deemed his *carne dejour,* spurred the hungery hunter in him. Spring loading his stance, he waited. A second later the chase was on.

Timothy Tabbis loved his new home. Now if he could only find a friend or two, it would be perfect.

One day, following the river under threatening skies, he entered the nearby hamlet of Gays Mills. As he walked down one of its quiet neighborhood streets, he paused to savor the fragrance of fresh cut grass and broad leaf maple trees. While lost in the charm of this valley hamlet he did not notice the three village cats now standing abreast in front of him.

The brawny one gruffly asked, "Hey! What's your name? Where'd you come from?" But, rudely, before Timothy Tabbis could answer, he continued, "I'm Jo, dis here's Buttercup and da scrawny one is Skinny."

With a polite tilt of his head Timothy Tabbis said, "How do you do Jo, Miss Buttercup, Skinny. My name is Timothy Tabbis."

Skinny, a tan Siamese, stammered, "Sa . . . sa . . . say what?" as his tail twitched.

Buttercup, a plump long-haired calico, fluttered her lengthy eyelashes with a flirtatious look over her ample shoulder, "You talk real proper for a cat with ears like those . . . " she paused, then winked, "But what are ears between friends Mister Tabbis?"

To be sure his words would be heard correctly Timothy Tabbis cleared his throat and in his best English said, "No. It's Timothy Tabbis, if you please." Then thinking of where he came from he said, "And yes, um . . . I come from across the pond . . . Britain."

Jo burst into a belly-hugging fit of laughter. "Will ya listen to dis guy," he bellowed. "He not only talks like he's from outer space, he thinks he can swim."

Buttercup giggled sarcastically, "And what's that thing sticking out from behind him? A tail?"

"Could've fooled me-me-me-me," stuttered Skinny.

Ignoring their rudeness Timothy Tabbis respectfully tried to explain.

"What I mean is," he began slowly. "Professor Bewilly and I fl ew-" but Timothy Tabbis stopped short as he looked into their bewilderedfaces and realized he was getting nowhere. Still, being one not to give up easily he went on. "You see humans can fly great distances in what they call the airplane," he lectured while the threesome's unfriendly glares became stares of total disbelief. Nonetheless he pressed on. "They pile themselves into it . . . " but he was loudly interrupted by a sudden thunderclap that cut the air with a piercing crack.

Jo dropped to the ground while Buttercup nervously looked about for a place to hide, and Skinny got the jitters so bad his entire body shook like a leaf. Slowly they began backing away from the golden newcomer when another thunderous boom bristled the hairs on their backs, sending them scrambling for cover as the first raindrops splattered the pavement.

But, like his father, Timothy Tabbis spent much of his time in the outdoors of the English countryside. And, like his father, he was a master of stealth, effortlessly bounding through deep snow, and relishing the coming of warm spring rain. Gleefully he trotted to the doorway, eave, and porch where Jo, Buttercup, and Skinny had crouched.

First to Buttercup, he said, "Come on lassie, don't let the rain catch you crying." She turned her back on him.

He skipped over to the porch and said, "Come on ole chap, take a trot on the wet side. It's quite invigorating, it'll be fun." But Skinny was shaking to hard to hear him.

And when he got to Jo, Jo hissed, "Goooo away . . . WEIRDO!"

Timothy Tabbis shrugged his shoulders and sighed, "Have it your way," then casually meandered out of town. And as he trotted away the rain stopped. Keeping beneath the cover of the underbrush he quietly secreted into the woodland's calm, taking the first path he crossed.

"Cats are fast, cats are quick," he sang, "cats jump higher than the pogo stick. Cats are clean with their furry sheen, sitting on the lap of an British Queen."

In the dark of the hollow log Randolph frightfully listened to the sing song words coming nearer and nearer. Squeezing his eyes shut, drawing his wings tight against his body, he waited.

The melodious song suddenly stopped and a voice said, "Hello."

Timothy Tabbis's whiskers had given a slight twitch as he passed the hollow log, which of course always prompted a look-see.

"Hello," he greeted again. When no answer came from the little ball of feathers, he thought perhaps he had interrupted a game of hide-n-seek, so he asked, "Are you hiding from someone?"

Opening one eye then the other, Randolph found himself

staring into the furry face of a very large creature, with green almond eyes that sparkled in the darkness.

"I said are you hiding from someone?" he asked again.

Shaking with fright Randolph could only stare at the big golden head.

Timothy Tabbis chuckled, and said, "Cat got your tongue?"

"Please don't eat me," he pleaded, as he backed himself deeper into the log.

"Oh dear, no, no, no," replied the cat. "My name is Timothy Tabbis. And yours?"

A small chirp echoed, "Ran . . . Randolph Rob . . . Robin, Mi . . . mi . . . ster Tabbis."

"Pleasure . . . but please, do call me Timothy Tabbis. I much prefer hearing my full name. There's something about Tabbis that gives Timothy more class. Don't you think?" he said with a Cheshire grin.

"I . . .guess . . . I guess so Mister . . . I mean Timothy . . . I mean Timothy Tabbis."

"Well Ran . . . Ran . . . Randolph Rob . . . Rob . . . Robin how do you do?"

"Randolph . . . just Randolph, sir," corrected the little robin.

"Aren't you feeling all stuffy and squashy back there? You look terribly uncomfortable," said Timothy Tabbis. "Oh please, do come out," he went on as he took a few steps back, "my legs are beginning to cramp."

Randolph did feel squashed and hot, and not knowing what to do, he cautiously hopped to the edge of the opening.

Timothy Tabbis's towering mass seem to fill the forest. His golden-yellow fur, sprinkled with flecks of white, carpeted his entire body except for his snow-white underside. Long auburn whiskers flanked his moist tan button nose that twitched now and then above a mouth filled with glistening white teeth that could be glimpsed when he spoke.

Attempting to put the little robin at ease he joked, "Do you happen to know what an airplane is?" And after a moment of silence he continued. "What are you doing down here?" His marble eyes darted here and there, as he added, "Didn't your parents tell you of the dangers lurking about down here?"

He raised his keen snout and gave a couple of sniffs before concluding, "Why a sly ole fox, hiding in a bush, would find you to be a tasty snack before dinner."

"Y . . . y . . . es," quivered Randolph, followed with a rapid-fire explanation. "You see my sister, her name is Ruby, and my brother, his name is Robby, and me, well we were flapping, then it was my turn, I was doing okay, then I fell I think grabity got me and then . . . "

Timothy Tabbis lifted a paw as if to stop an oncoming car, and said, "Slow down, slow down, I can barely keep up." He sat upon his haunches and spoke very slowly, "The word is gra . . . vi . . . ty, my dear boy. Now please continue, I'm all ears."

"Yes, that's what my father called it. You see, Ruby and Robby," he continued tearfully, "are already flying, and all I can do is fall over."

Turning to show his tail, he went on, "Because I don't have much for tail feathers. Now I'm stuck down here on the ground and I'll never get back home."

Timothy Tabbis reached out with a gentle arm and coaxed Randolph closer to him. "Cheer up ole boy. If that's all you're worried about you have more than you realize to be thankful for." And while drawing circles on the dirt path he said, "I've seen birds with lesser tails than yours fly circles around the best of them."

Randolph wiped away his tears, and asked, "Even Pauline?"

Raising an inquisitive brow he asked, "And who may I ask is Pauline?"

"She lives in the old elm tree."

"Oh! No doubt about it!" Timothy Tabbis replied, as he playfully swatted at a pair of butterflies fluttering by. "She might as well be tied to a stone when these little birdies take to the sky."

Randolph was imagining tailless birds flying high in the sky when Timothy Tabbis, with a big lovable smile said, "I guess you're lucky I found you."

The little robin was beginning to believe his good fortune, and though the towering mass of golden-yellow fur could gobble him up in one bite, he sensed Timothy Tabbis was not the kind of animal his father described. Still the question begged to be asked.

"Does that mean you're not going to . . . to . . . eat me?"

"For heaven sakes no," the big cat proclaimed, "and, frankly speaking my dear boy, I would find it a bit," he paused, cleared his throat, and said, "distasteful."

Raising his large paw, from which a razor-sharp claw appeared, he gently lifted one of Randolph's feathers. "Its the feathers. They'd catch between my teeth and drive me absolutely bonkers."

Then he bent down inches from the little bird and whispered, "You see my dear fellow, mice are my *carne de jour.*"

Randolph wanted to ask what mice were but remained silent as the large cat went on. "Night will be here all too soon, and things will get rather dicey down here. Besides, if I found you so easily you are sure to be discovered by a less civilized creature. And believe you me they won't be singing do-dol-le-do."

"What about my family?" whimpered Randolph, "I want to go home."

Timothy Tabbis looked up into the dense canopy knowing that any one of the thousands of branches could be Randolph's home. But which one?

He kindly patted him on the back, and said, "Buck up Randolph, there's nothing we can do at the moment. It'll be dark soon and we must get you out of harm's way. I know just the spot. Now stick close and don't get to far behind."

Randolph asked, "Do you think I'll ever get back home?"

"It may take a little time but, yes, you'll find your way home," he assured him. "However, in the meantime you'll find me to be a cat of culture. I'm meticulously clean and a wonderful conversationalist," he boasted.

Randolph had no ideal what meticulous or a conversationalist meant, but the big cat's shimmering green eyes, soft golden-yellow fur, and jolly way of speaking made him feel safe. As they walked Timothy Tabbis made up a new song.

"As I was walking through the forest one day, on a sunny, sunny day of May, when I found a little fellow, hiding in a hollow, who said he'd lost his way."

The big cat kept a steady pace, making frequent stops to listen and sniff the air, or glance over his shoulder to make sure Randolph had not gotten tangled in the ivy or lost in the brambles. These brief stops gave Randolph a chance to rest and observe the cat more closely. He soon noticed something about Timothy Tabbis that did not fit his father's description of cats. It was something that made Randolph think that maybe cats and birds were not so different after all. He decided to ask Timothy Tabbis about it the next time they stopped.

Coming to the edge of a meadow Timothy Tabbis stopped. His button nose tested the air for danger before choosing a large boulder to rest upon.

Randolph thought this would be a great time to ask his burning question. "Timothy Tabbis, may I ask you a something?"

"Yes, you may."

"I was wondering why you don't have a long slender tail. Father said cats have long slender tails and yours is . . . well . . . short . . . and stubby."

"Well, not all cats," he began. "You see my daddy was an authentic wild cat, a Bobcat." He made a slight giggle when he added, "It was quite the event when mummy, a well-heeled house cat, and daddy got together."

"What does that have to do with your tail?" asked Randolph.

Timothy Tabbis paused for a second thinking of his tabby mother. "My dear old mum said I was his spittin' image. They, bobcats, all have short tails, long legs, pointy ears, and big paws. All of which I have except for the legs, got me mum's legs."

"Where do you and your mom live?" Randolph asked.

"Oh, she's not with me anymore."

Randolph looked puzzled. "Where was she? I didn't see her?"

"No, not with us now," Timothy Tabbis sighed, "she has passed on, you know . . . she's gone."

After a few seconds of quiet Randolph got it.

"So where do you live?" he repeated.

"I live with a wonderful and very smart human named . . . "

Randolph cut him off before he finished. "What are humans?" he blurted, "and can you still do cat things, even with your tail like that?"

Timothy Tabbis had stopped listening. His pointy ears angled forward as he rose upon his large paws, and said in a hushed voice, "We must leave at once."

He jumped to the ground keeping his sharp eyes focused on the movement lurking in the tall grass. "There's a fox on the prowl."

Randolph paid no attention to the warning. He wanted to know more about the big cat. "But will it grow?" he persisted.

"The answer to your questions will have to wait my dear fellow. Right now we must keep moving. We still have a long way to go before you're safe."

Chapter 4

Their Loss

Pattie said, "We have enough, let's go home."

"Yes, no telling what those little ones have gotten into," grinned Pete.

Ruby and Robby stood side-by-side with their heads down as their parents landed next to the nest.

"Where's Randolph?" Pattie demanded.

Ruby stepped forward. "We were practicing and . . . " she glanced over at Robby twiddling the tips of his wings while staring at his feet. "He fell!" she cried.

Pattie gasped and Pete immediately flew off in search of him.

"Have you seen a small robin?" he asked a grazing deer. "He's about this tall and has a stubby tail." But the doe had not.

He came upon his old friend Charlie the squirrel, and asked, "Have you seen Randolph, Charlie?"

"Why, yes I have," he chattered. "It was about two days ago . . . "

"No . . . no . . . no . . . today, have you seen him today?"

"Nope," replied Charlie.

After hours of searching Pete sorrowfully flew back to his nest.

Drowned in thought he did not hear his neighbors, Pauline and Myrtle, cackling back and forth.

Pauline had called over to her friend, perched on a branch, grooming her feathers, and said, "Let's go find something to eat."

As Pauline turned to take off Myrtle snapped, "What? Wait! Why do you always have to be the one to go first?" "Just because you said lets go doesn't mean . . . "

Pauline huffily pulled her wings in and retorted, "Because you're too slow girl. First you have to prune your feathers, fluff your crown, and make sure the wind's blowin' in the right direction." Rolling her eyes she ended, "And besides, I'm older."

"Well, you got me there," said Myrtle. "How does that saying go? Oh yeah, I remember. Age before beauty."

Pauline scowled and said, "Girl, who you callin . . . "

Myrtle cut her off. "Oh, don't get all riled up Pauline. But you have to admit, I am smarter."

Pauline's irritating scowl turned to a sly old smile. "Huh! I'll admit to that when I see you flyin' backwards."

When they saw Pete they stopped their bantering.

Pete landed on a nearby branch, and asked, "Pauline, Myrtle, have you seen Randolph?"

"The one with the stubby tail feathers?" asked Pauline.

"Yes, that's Randolph. He fell out of the nest. Have you seen him?"

"My heavens! No, I haven't," she said.

"Me neither," said Myrtle.

"He can't be far," said Pete.

"What are you going to do?" asked Pauline. "A little guy like him, down there . . . ?"

"I know," sighed Pete.

Throughout the nights that followed their loss, Pete and Pattie remained hopeful they would hear the familiar chirp of their beloved. Even bfefore the sun crest the horizon they were out combing the nearby hills and meadows.

One night Ruby asked, "Mommy, will we ever see Randolph again?"

Pattie could barely hold back her tears. She believed that somehow Randolph would find his way home. "Yes, if we never give up hope," she answered as she stroked her daughter's head. "I wouldn't be surprised if he's having the time of his life. What do you think?"

Ruby did not answer. She had fallen into a dream, a dream of racing her brothers under sun-soaked clouds drifting across a brilliant blue sky.

Chapter 5

The Grassy Divide

With every passing hour the distance between Randolph and his family increased. Timothy Tabbis had rescued him from unknown dangers, and had given Randolph no reasons to fear him, at least not until they crossed the grassy divide.

Timothy Tabbis suddenly turned to Randolph, and whispered, "Don't move Randolph. Whatever you do, don't move."

"What is it?" asked Randolph.

The big cat did not answer, instead he quietly inched ahead, halting every few steps before moving onward. Randolph stood as tall as he could to see what had grabbed the cat's interest. Then with lightning speed Timothy Tabbis sprang from his crouched stance and burst into long, fluid strides, changing direction at the drop of a hat.

Tuffs of tall grass and random clumps of thistles made it difficult for Randolph to keep track of the cat's wild movements. Then out of the blue a frantic mouse zipped passed him huffing and puffing screaming, "RUNNNN . . . RUN FOR YOUR LIFE!!!"

Randolph wasted no time in taking off in the opposite direction as fast as his little robin legs could carry him. Before he got very far a powerful blow knocked him off his feet. Dazed, he struggled to right himself but found he was pinned by two large paws.

Squeezing his eyes shut he chirped at the top of his lungs, "HELP! HELP!"

He forced himself to take a quick glance, in hopes of seeing his friend coming to his rescue. Instead he looked into the fiery eyes of . . .

"No! It's me . . . it's me . . . it's me, Timothy Tabbis," he screamed.

The big golden tabby shook his head, as if he had not a clue as to the events that had just unfolded. Yet, the thunderous pounding of his little friend's heart, the clatter of his wobbling legs, and rattle of his quivering wings told a grim story. Timothy Tabbis backed away and again shook his head to clear his mind.

"Randolph, are you okay?"

Randolph peeked over his quaking wings into the twinkling eyes of the big cat. But all he could see was the grizzly monster that had chased and knocked him over, and he fainted. When he awoke Timothy Tabbis was stretched out beside him, smiling. Randolph jumped to his feet ready to run away.

"I'm sorry, Randolph," said Timothy Tabbis softly.

"Youuu were gonna . . . gonna eat me," shouted Randolph.

The yellow cat bowed his head, and said, "You have every right to be angry at me. It all happened so quickly. I didn't realize it was you."

Randolph was still not convinced as he stammered on. "You said you . . . don don don't . . . eat birds. Next time . . . I cou-cou-could be a goner."

Timothy Tabbis thought of how terrifying it must have been for Randolph, not to mention how close he came to . . . he couldn't finish the thought. He agreed.

"Point well taken, Randolph. We'll have to devise a way to keep you out of the action when I'm on the hunt." He paused to wipe his nose and then continued, "I could never forgive myself if something were to happen to you."

Even though Randolph's confidence had been shaken he believed the big golden cat. "Promise me it will never happen again Timothy Tabbis. Promise."

"I promise," the big cat smiled, "I promise my little friend. I promise with all my lives."

Feeling a catnap coming on Timothy Tabbis lazily rolled over onto his back and stared into the blue. His eyes were mere slits when Randolph hopped upon his chest.

"Teach me how. I mean, could you teach me how to run as fast as you?" Implored Randolph.

"Gladly, but you're missing two important things," Timothy Tabbis said drowsily.

"What two things?" Randolph asked.

"Two more legs," replied Timothy Tabbis.

"Oh twitters," Randolph groaned, "I'll never grow two more legs."

"Listen lad, you're a flyer not a runner," said Timothy Tabbis. "But I think I know where you're going with this."

He glanced up at the sky then went on. "The thing about hunters is that they chase whatever moves. If they do not see the object moving it's as though it's just another bush or stone lying on the ground."

"That's not very smart," said Randolph.

Timothy Tabbis smirked at the notion, and replied, "Well, let's just say it's nature's way of leveling the playing field."

Thinking of his near-death experience, Randolph said, "So, if I had stayed put, you would have run right by me?"

"Precisely," answered Timothy Tabbis.

"You're joking," Randolph giggled.

With a straight face Timothy Tabbis said, "If I'm joking, I can fly."

He was about to suggest they get on their way, when Randolph broke into a fit of laughter.

Looking slightly irritated Timothy Tabbis asked, "What's so funny?"

"A flying cat!" Randolph managed to blurt out before tumbling off the furry mountain.

"Dear me. Aren't you the funny one," smiled the big cat.

Chapter 6

The Hidden Grotto

Keeping to the shadows of the thick underbrush, the pair was exhausted by the time they came upon the banks of a rushing stream.

"I can't go any farther," complained Randolph.

"You don't have to. We're here! This is it," announced Timothy Tabbis.

"This?" chirped a confused Randolph.

"Yes," said Timothy Tabbis, "that's what makes this the perfect hideaway. You can't see it unless you know it's here."

The gush of bubbling water grew louder as Randolph's puzzled look turned to disbelief. "You mean, you want me to hide in there?" he gulped, pointing at the brook.

"No, no, no, you silly bird. You're no duck," said Timothy Tabbis.

Looking up he continued, "Your new home, for the time being, is up there."

Hidden by a rocky outcrop, Timothy Tabbis's secret place was a small cave nestled in the high cliffs overlooking the brook. However, getting Randolph up the uneven ground would require some thought. Then an idea came to him.

"And to get you up there I will carry you."

Randolph wasn't sure what this meant but he trusted that his furry friend knew what he was doing. Still, as the cat opened his mouth to pick him up, Randolph let out a blood-curdling scream that sent Timothy Tabbis backward landing on his rear.

After regaining his footing and shaking the dirt from his backside, Timothy Tabbis patiently explained, "Listen, when I was a wee lad like you, mummy, bless her soul, carried me like this all the time. So let's get on with it. Now hold very still."

He gently placed his mouth around the tiny bird and swiftly bounded up the steep climb, over boulders and fallen trees, until he reached the outcrop. Cautiously approaching the entrance of the cave he released his precious cargo.

"Now that wasn't so bad, was it?" he asked, as he sat down for a much-needed rest.

"Nope," replied Randolph, ruffling his feathers, "but could you hold back on the wet stuff next time?"

"The next time old fellow," chuckled Timothy Tabbis, "you'll be carrying me."

They both laughed at the thought, but Randolph's laughter soon gave way to the growling and rumbling of hunger. Since their journey began he had not eaten much, an ant here, an ant there, but certainly not enough to satisfy him.

"I'm so hungry," began Randolph, "I could eat a . . ."

"Mouse!" blurted Timothy Tabbis.

"Yuck!" Randolph said, "Robins don't eat mice."

"Then how about a froggie or fishie?" teased Timothy Tabbis.

"Yuck, that's disgusting too!" said Randolph.

Timothy Tabbis then playfully said, "How could I be so insensitive? You robins don't eat meat. You're an insectarian."

"What's a insec . . . insect," Randolph sputtered.

"Insec . . . tarian," Timothy Tabbis said slowly, "are those who eat bugs and worms." He shuddered at the thought.

Randolph could see and taste each of them. "Yes. That's what I am . . . would you please, please find me some of those things?"

"Oh, dear boy, one please is good enough," said Timothy Tabbis, as he strolled out of the cave. "Stay put, and remember to say *thank you* when I return."

He was not gone long before returning with a mouthfull of berries and insects, but before Randolph could say *thank you* he was off again. Upon his second return he held a succulent fish flapping between his teeth. The two companions ate until their bellies were full. After finishing their meals Timothy Tabbis lazily licked his jowls, and yawned as he curled into a mountain of fur.

Feeling content and safe, Randolph nuzzled up against his friend's purring warmth, and in the coolness of their grotto the pair fell asleep.

Chapter 7

Battle and Victory

A large mango sun hung just above the forest canopy casting a golden hue upon the rocky face of the outcrop and through the opening of the cave. Randolph and Timothy Tabbis slept soundly under the cover of the cave's dim coolness, yet the cat's keen ears, always on alert, picked up the sound of something moving about. Opening one eye, he caught the sight of a long slithering form stalking in the shadows.

Lightly nudging Randolph, as not to startle him, he whispered, "Wake up Randolph, we have a visitor."

"Who is it," Randolph yawned.

"Shhh. Not so loud. It's a snake," said Timothy Tabbis, under his breath.

Randolph had no idea what a snake was. Snakes had not been on Father's list of dangerous creatures. "Should I invite him in for a little lunch?" Randolph whispered.

"If you do, you'll be the lunch," said Timothy Tabbis, as he sprang to his feet as the hair on the back of his neck bristled.

His kind lovable voice changed to a rumbling growl followed by a long hiss, as he cautiously circled the intruder. The rattle of the snake's tail warned of its intent. In the blink of an eye it lunged with lightening quickness. Its jaws poised to deliver its deadly venom. Equally the big cat sprang forward with claws at the ready. Timothy Tabbis released a roar so loud the walls of the small cave seem to shake. He side stepped the attacker just in time to lock his powerful sharp teeth behind the snakes head. Dust and stones spewed skyward as the two enemies flipped and flailed from one end of the cave to the other.

Randolph could only watch as Timothy Tabbis fought for their lives; the snake tightly coiled around the feline's flexing muscles; the cat's teeth deep into the serpent's flesh. The fight twisted into a ball of golden-yellow fur and glistening scales to the very edge of the outcrop, and then they fell from sight.

Randolph stood in disbelief. Seconds later, Timothy Tabbis emerged sporting a victorious smile. Randolph rushed to his side and wrapped his wings around a strong furry leg.

Exhausted, Timothy Tabbis said wearily, "Now where was I?" Then as though recalling something misplaced, he said, "Oh yes, I remember." He then leisurely lay down and said, "Randolph, do sleep well."

Randolph shuddered at the thought of sleep and yelled, "How can I sleep with monsters creeping in here? In the nest we were safe," he sniffled.

The soft light that seeped into the cave showed the speckled markings of Randolph's changing colors. Timothy Tabbis clearly understood Randolph's fears. He remembered being a frightened kitten and how his own shadow could scare him. He remembered how his mother would tuck him close to her and whisper, "Have no fear my dear, I will always be here."

Timothy Tabbis's glowing green eyes blinked in the semi darkness, and as he drew Randolph close to him he said, "Have no fear Randolph, I will always be here. Now go to sleep."

"But what if you fall asleep?" Randolph said worriedly.

Sitting ramrod straight like a king on his throne, a lion before his pride, Timothy Tabbis replied, "But I won't."

Chapter 8

Time to Fly

After countless missions gathering food for his little friend, Timothy Tabbis had come to the conclusion it was time for Randolph to learn to fly. He remembered the words Professor Bewilly whispered the morning they left for America, "Journey, just another word for adventure." He too had been away from home long enough, and that this journey, this adventure, should come to an end. He waited until Randolph had finished his evening meal of grasshopper, worms, and berries to suggest his plan.

"Randolph old chap, I think it's time you start pursuing your dream."

With a beak full of berries, Randolph sputtered, "Whaa . . . drom ar yu alkin abot?"

Surprised that he actually understood what the little fellow said, Timothy Tabbis firmly admonished, "Randolph, manners are a necessity which one cannot forgo. Regurgitating your dinner when speaking goes against all civilized rules of communication."

"Whaaa?" Randolph replied.

"Swallow before speaking."

"Oh," Randolph gulped. "What dream?"

"The dream of going home," said Timothy Tabbis. "It's time you started learning to fly."

"I . . . but . . . I don't think I can. Every time I tried before, I fell over," chirped Randolph.

"That was then, this is now," said Timothy Tabbis. "And besides, you have a wonderful family waiting for you. Don't you want to see them again?"

Looking up at his friend, Randolph said, "You're my family now, Timothy Tabbis."

Although he felt the same, and had grown close to Randolph, he knew this was best.

"Don't worry Randolph, we'll always be best mates," he said.

His auburn whiskers twitched above snow-white teeth as he went on. "Just imagine how far we'll go, and all the new sights we'll see once you're flying."

Then with a big smile he chuckled, "And I'll be free of having to catch those pesky little grubs you call a meal."

As Timothy Tabbis spoke Randolph imagined the two of them scaling mountains, fighting off dangerous creatures, and discovering unknown lands.

Randolph was up as the first rays of sunlight dripped into the cave's dimness. He stretched his wings and pruned an out of place feather. He felt strangely different as he puffed his now pumpkin orange chest, balanced his tail feathers, and began flapping. Within seconds he rose from the cave floor. It was time for Randolph to take the Big Plunge.

He hopped into the open air beaming with pride. He fanned his wings and took a few practice hops while yelling at the top of his lungs,

"Timothy Tabbis . . . hurry . . . come . . . come."

The big cat trotted over to see his little friend flapping and hopping.

"Today is the day," Randolph said.

Timothy Tabbis hugged a large stone and proclaimed, "If it weren't for this boulder, you'd blow me right over."

For the first time in Randolph's life he felt like a robin, a true robin, a master of the sky. He lifted his chest high and grandly flaaped his wings.

Standing on the cliff's edge he repeated, "I can do it, I can do it. It's now or never," he breathed.

"Nowwww," whispered Timothy Tabbis.

To   Randolph that whisper was like a gust of wind pushing him off the cliff into the unknown. But, as the whosh of air surrounded him the ghost of his past failures caused him to doubt his abilities. Fear drowned out Timothy Tabbis's plea to *spread your wings* as a blur of brown and green hurled up at him. Time was running out, and with only seconds remaining, his life seem to flash before him: his mother and father, Ruby and Robby, and smiling emerald eyes. Then his father's words came to him *if it had wings it would fly*. And with no time to spare he spread his wings, swooping inches above the ground.

Making his first right turn was scary, but he quickly learned to shift from right to left with ease. He stroked his wings harder, lifting himself higher into the sky. Randolph could see farther than he ever imagined, over treetops, hilltops, and across the distant horizon to the Kickcapoo River. The wind coursed faster and faster over his wings, filling him with excitement and pride.

Using the golden cat as his marker he readied for his first landing. As he closed in on his target, doubt once again rose up inside him. But before Randolph could think another thought his tail feathers fanned out and he smoothly landed a few steps in front of his friend.

The big cat strolled over to Randolph, his heart a bit heavy. He wished they could remain as they were, carefree and happy. Yet to see his friend grown up and flying was worth it all.

"Well . . . I guess, Maylene . . . "

"Mrytle," corrected Randolph.

"I guess she's got nothing on you," continued Timothy Tabbis.

But before he could utter another word, Randolph took to the skies, calling down to his earth bound friend, "No! She doesn't. I have the wind at my back and a great set of tail feathers to steer me in."

Chapter 9

Reunion

Ruby and Robby were out on a morning breakfast search.

"Hello Ruby. Hello Robby. Any luck on breakfast?" It was their neighbors Pauline and Myrtle.

"Not yet, how about you?" they replied.

"The fields are being plowed," said Myrtle.

"You'll find all the worms and grubs you can eat," added Pauline.

"But hurry before it gets too crowded," warned Myrtle.

"Thanks for the tip," Ruby said, as they made a sharp turn toward the fields. Pauline was right; the black soil was teeming with worms and grubs. Robby and Ruby feasted until a black cloud of noisy starlings swooped down.

Robby called to his sister, "Why don't we take a couple of worms to mom and dad. It might cheer them up."

"Good idea," she replied, "they could use a little cheering up."

Each clutching a worm, they flew off.

Ruby and Roby were not far from home when they thought they heard someone call their names. With a quick glance over their shoulders they saw nothing. Seconds later a blur whizzed by them, circling in stunning figure eights before settling into a parallel flight along side them.

"Hey! What do you think you're doing?" yelled Robby.

"That wasn't very polite," scolded Ruby.

"Sorry guys, I thought you were someone I knew," said the stranger as he flew ahead.

At first neither Ruby nor Robby recognized him, but as the distance widened between them Ruby noticed something familiar. She increased her speed to get a better look.

"Randolph!" she screeched. "Look Robby . . . it's Randolph! It's Randolph!"

The three landed on the first branch they came to.

"Is it really you?" twittered Robby.

Randolph turned, and proudly displayed his short stubby tail.

Beaming, Ruby said, "My dream has come true."

"What did you dream?" asked Randolph.

"That one day we would race under a blue sky filled with sun-soaked clouds," she cheerfully chirped.

"Did you dream I was the fastest?" teased Randolph, before taking off like a shot.

Pattie was perched on the branch of their maple tree when Pete landed along side her.

"Pattie, I just over heard a couple of guinea hens talking about the oddest thing," he began. "They spotted a cat and small bird traveling together, the day Randolph fell from the nest. They said the little bird was walking alongside the big cat as though it had nothing to fear."

"Did they say what kind of bird?" Pattie asked, paying no attention to the strangeness of the scene Pete had just described.

"The same question crossed my mind," he replied.

"And!"

He shrugged his shoulders, and said, "If there's one thing guinea hens are not good at, it's details. Poor eyesight."

"Oh Pete, what if that little bird was our Randolph," Pattie said with the hope only a mother could express.

"Pattie, do you really believe a cat, of all animals . . . it's just not possible. Don't get your hopes up," he sighed.

"If I do not hope for the impossible then the possible may never happen," she answered.

"Mom! Dad!" a trio of chirps rang from above.

Pete and Pattie looked up to see three winged dots flying toward them. Not until they were right upon them did Pattie recognize Randolph.

Opening her wings to receive him, he smoothly landed before her.

"Oh Randolph," she said as she and Pete, Ruby and Robby hugged him tightly.

"Mom, Dad," Randolph began, "I missed you so much." He looked at his father and said, "Dad you won't believe what I found out about cats."

Randolph was still telling them about his adventures as the daytime shade of their maple tree turned into evening shadows. He told them how Timothy Tabbis found him in the hollow log, and that he didn't eat birds because he hated plucking feathers from between his teeth. He described the great battle and victory over the snake, and how the kindly tabby cat had encouraged him to not give up on his dream to fly.

That night a glimmering white crescent moon glimmered in an inky black sky as the Robin family settled in for the night. Randolph gazed longingly into the warm night air. Already he was missing the melodious charm of Timothy Tabbis's cheerful voice, and, for a second, he thought he heard the big cat somewhere below. Then out of the darkness appeared two glowing eyes. Their silent promise of trust and friendship danced among the iridescent flickering of fireflies gliding through the blackness.

Randolph quietly called out, "Is that you?" Although the dancing eyes did not answer Randolph knew to whom they belonged. "I know it's you Timothy Tabbis," he whispered. "Thanks for everything. Without you I never would have made it home." He paused. "When will I see . . . ?"

But before his last words left his beak the glowing eyes vanished into the night, as a familiar voice echoed from afar. "Until our next adventure Randolph Robin! Until our next adventure!"

Professor Bewilly sat in his big leather chair facing the window as the morning rose above the Kickapoo River Valley. The sky was a deep lake blue when Timothy Tabbis arrived on the window's ledge. He jumped onto the professor's lap and curled himself into a pool of golden fur. The trill of his purr murmured softly as his friend's gentle fingers combed through his lush coat.

Professor Bewilly yawned, and said, "Good morning my dear old friend. Good to have you home again."